秘密花園

The Secret Garden

作者 Frances H. Burnett
改寫 Andrew Chien
審定 Dennis Le Boeuf／Liming Jing
譯者 鄭家文

Contents

🎧 **Preface**   3

1 **Leaving for Yorkshire** 前往約克郡   6

2 **Exploring the Manor** 在莊園的冒險   17

3 **The Secret Garden** 揭開秘密花園的面紗   27

4 **Getting to Know Dickon** 新朋友迪肯   37

5 **The Crying Sound at Night** 夜半的啜泣聲   45

6 **Colin's Rage** 憤怒的柯林   53

7 **The Determined Colin** 柯林的決心   59

8 **Mr. Craven's Big Surprise** 克雷文先生的大驚喜   68

Exercises   74
Translation   81
Answers   95

Preface

About the author

Frances Hodgson Burnett was born on November 24, 1849 in Manchester, England. After her father's death, her family moved to the U.S. in 1865.

When her mother died in 1870, Frances thought that she might be able to earn a living as a writer because she had always loved writing. She began writing romantic stories for magazines.

Frances Hodgson Burnett
(1849-1924)

Her work was well received by the public, but it wasn't until she published *Little Lord Fauntleroy*, her first children's book, in 1886 that she attained a lasting fame.

Her later works including *The Secret Garden* (1888) and *A Little Princess* (1909) are what she is best known for today. Frances Hodgson Burnett was married twice and became a U.S. citizen in 1905. She died on October 29, 1924.

About the characters

Mary Lennox	was born in India. She was nine years old and had a very bad temper until she moved to her uncle's house.
Kamala	was Mary's servant in India. She took care of Mary, because Mary's parents were very busy.
Mr. Archibald Craven	was Mary's uncle. Mr. Craven was described as "a miserable hunchback." Since his wife died, he had traveled a lot and had hardly seen his son, Colin.
Colin	was Mr. Craven's son. He thought he would become a hunchback and die an early death.
Mrs. Medlock	was Mr. Archibald Craven's housekeeper. She had taken care of Colin since Colin's mother died.
Martha	was a maid in the Cravens' residence. She was Dickon's sister.
Ben Weatherstaff	was an old gardener. He tended the Cravens' gardens.
Dickon	was Martha's brother. He enjoyed playing with the animals on the moor.

About the story

Mary Lennox was a bad-tempered, selfish girl. At the age of nine, her parents died during an epidemic and she was taken to live with her uncle, Mr. Archibald Craven, in Yorkshire, England. Although she lived in her uncle's house, she hardly saw him.

In the beginning, she hated everything about Yorkshire, but with the care and friendliness of the people and animals there, she began to reach out to everyone. However, she found that there seemed to be some sorrowful secrets about her uncle's house.

First, there was a secret, desolate garden in which her aunt died. Then there was a sick, bedridden boy in the house who turned out to be her cousin. However, with her care and dedication, Mary transformed the secret garden and even her cousin's health.

Finally, when Mr. Craven came home from a long trip in Europe, he found one more secret about the house. But the secret, this time, was an exceptionally cheerful one.

Leaving for Yorkshire

Mary Lennox was born in India. She was nine years old and had a thin angry face and thin yellow hair.

Her family wasn't as united as everyone else's. Her father was a British official with great assets[1] in India. Mary rarely saw her father, because, as a politician, he was always extremely occupied with his work. As a typical British official, his family was secondary to his career.

Mary's mother was a liberal[2], yet attractive beauty. She couldn't take care of her daughter, either, because she was only interested in getting a permanent[3] or going to parties.

---

1 asset ['æset] (n.) 資產；財產
2 liberal ['lɪbərəl] (n.) 自由主義者
3 permanent ['pɜːrmənənt] (n.) 〔口〕燙髮

🎧2 Hence, an Indian servant, Kamala, was appointed[4] to take care of Mary.

In fact, Mary was not different from her parents. Each person in the family only cared about himself or herself.

Mary only thought about her own needs and always gave orders to Kamala. As a servant, Kamala could only comply[5] with her naturally bad-tempered little mistress's demand.

✓ *Check Up* *Choose the correct answer.*

_____ 1. In terms of his profession, which of the following best describes Mary's father?
Ⓐ An ideal politician.
Ⓑ A researcher of distinction.
Ⓒ A long-term spokesman for a British enterprise.

4 appoint [ə'pɔɪnt] (v.) 任命；委派職務
5 comply [kəm'plaɪ] (v.) 順從；遵從

On a hot morning, Mary found out the daily delivery[6] of her breakfast was performed by a different servant.

"What are you doing here? Go bring Kamala to me!" Mary said angrily to the servant.

"Sorry, Miss Lennox. I'm afraid Kamala couldn't come," answered the servant with dismay[7].

"I hate Kamala! I'll kick her real hard when I see her," Mary threatened.

Afterwards, she saw her mother come to the garden with a man. The two adults didn't see Mary there, but Mary overheard their conversation.

6 delivery [dɪ'lɪvərɪ] (n.) 送東西來；傳送
7 dismay [dɪs'meɪ] (n.) 沮喪；氣餒

🎧4 Mary learned that there was a severe[8] epidemic[9] around town. Many people had either died or run away. She heard that Kamala had died of the epidemic, too.

Upon hearing that, she got very afraid. Sometimes she'd cry to herself; sometimes she'd try to slumber[10] away her fear. However, it seemed that her fear could last forever.

✔️*Check Up* *Choose the correct answer.*

_____ 2. What happened to Kamala?
    Ⓐ She was sent to a concentration camp.
    Ⓑ She was a victim of the epidemic.
    Ⓒ She was promoted.

8 severe [sɪ'vɪr] (a.) 嚴重的
9 epidemic [ˌɛpɪ'dɛmɪk] (n.) 流行傳染病
10 slumber ['slʌmbər] (v.) 睡眠

One day Mary woke up to find the house quiet. There was no servant by her bed. Then she heard men's voices from the hall.

"I really feel sorry for the Lennox family. It was pure bad luck," said one voice.

"There was a child, too. None of us ever saw her. Where is the pitiful child?" said the other.

Suddenly, Mary opened the door to meet them. The two men were surprised at first, and then they showed great sympathy[11] for her.

"Poor girl! Your parents both died of the disease. All of your servants ran away."

Mary didn't miss her parents, for she was not familiar with them. She only thought of herself. "Where will I live?" she asked.

Unlike many other orphans[12], Mary wasn't sent to some charity foundation[13]. Instead, she was informed she would be taken back to England. Moreover, she would live with her uncle, Mr. Archibald Craven, a man of great substance[14] and reputation[15] in suburban Yorkshire.

Mary never heard of such an uncle. She didn't know she had relatives in England. She didn't even know where Yorkshire was located. She just hoped the uncle was nice and would permit her to do anything she wanted.

 *Check Up* Choose the correct answer.

_____ 3. Mary was emotional about her parents' death.   (True) (False)

---

11 sympathy ['sɪmpəθi] (n.) 同情
12 orphan ['ɔːrfən] (n.) 孤兒
13 charity foundation 慈善基金會
14 substance ['sʌbstəns] (n.) 財產
15 reputation [ˌrepjʊ'teɪʃən] (n.) 名譽；聲望

Upon her arrival in England with loads[16] of luggage, Mary was met by Mrs. Medlock, her uncle's housekeeper, at the port. Mrs. Medlock was a conservative[17] elderly woman with a strong faith[18] in religion.

She had a red face and brilliant[19] black eyes. Her tone of speech reminded Mary of her father's friend, a reprimanding[20] justice of the federal court[21] from Australia.

Mary didn't like her, and Mrs. Medlock didn't like Mary, either.

"Are you my servant?" Mary asked.

Check Up *Choose the correct answer.*

_____ 4. Mary thought Mrs. Medlock was her servant.　(True) (False)

16 load [loʊd] (n.) 裝載（量）
17 conservative [kənˈsɜːrvətɪv] (a.) 保守的；傳統的
18 faith [feɪθ] (n.) 信仰
19 brilliant [ˈbrɪljənt] (a.) 光亮的
20 reprimand [ˈreprɪmænd] (v.) 訓斥；譴責
21 federal court 聯邦法院

"You'd better watch your manners," said Mrs. Medlock disapprovingly. "I only work for Mr. Craven. I'm responsible for the internal administration of the Cravens' residence[22]. I'm also his deputy[23] when he's away. Anyway, I was told to bring you to Yorkshire. Hurry up! We need to catch the two p.m. train."

On the train, Mary silently watched the landscape out of the window. Although Mary left Mrs. Medlock with a somewhat disagreeable impression and seemed to need some discipline[24], Mrs. Medlock tried to talk to Mary.

🎧9 "Your uncle lives in an enormous old manor[25] near the county border. It has roughly a hundred rooms, but most of them were locked. The manor also features all kinds of gardens and finely decorated columns. What do you think of that?"

"I don't care," Mary said dismissively[26].

"You are such an odd child. Well, that's OK. Although Mr. Craven will fund your living expenses in Yorkshire, I bet he won't necessarily care about you, either. He stays mostly in his room and never spends time with anyone. He does not even go to the polls[27]. He is a crooked[28] man with vast wealth. He had never smiled until he got married."

✓Check Up *Choose the correct answer.*

_____ 5. Which of the following best illustrates Mr. Archibald Craven's accommodations?
　Ⓐ A conventional cottage.
　Ⓑ A contemporary apartment.
　Ⓒ A large country house.

22　residence ['rezɪdəns] (n.) 官邸
23　deputy ['depjʊti] (n.) 代理人
24　discipline ['dɪsɪplɪn] (n.) 紀律
25　manor ['mænər] (n.) 莊園
26　dismissively [dɪs'mɪsɪvli] (adv.) 不屑一顧地
27　poll [poʊl] (n.) 投票
28　crooked ['krʊkɪd] (a.) 駝背的

🎧10 "He's married?" Mary sounded surprised.

"He was married. Mrs. Craven died a decade ago."

"She died?" Mary found the story intriguing[29].

"Oh, yes. Now Mr. Craven doesn't seem to care about anything. He locks himself up in his room all day and sees nobody. He won't want to see you, either. So, you'd better behave yourself and do what you're told to do."

Although there was no need to transfer, the nonstop train journey took almost a day. When they reached Yorkshire, it was already dark. It was a cold and windy night. Mary thought it was very different from India.

✓ *Check Up* *Choose the correct answer.*

_____ 6. Mary and Mrs. Medlock took a transfer train before reaching Yorkshire. (True) (False)

29 intriguing [ɪnˈtriːgɪŋ] (a.) 激起興趣的

2 Exploring the Manor

When Mary and Mrs. Medlock arrived at the manor, they were both tired. Mary was immediately taken upstairs to her room. In her room, there was a warm fire and food on the table.

"This is your room," said Mrs. Medlock. "Finish your dinner and go to bed. Don't go wandering around the house. If you want to live here, you'd better follow the regulations[1]."

---

1 regulation [ˌrɛɡjʊˈleɪʃən] (n.) 規章

When Mary woke up the next morning, she saw a servant cleaning her room. The servant was a lean young woman with rosy cheeks.

"Who are you?"

"My name is Martha, miss," said the maid cheerfully.

Mary looked through the net curtains by the window and saw an expansive field. There were no trees or houses. She asked Martha, "What's that out there?"

"It's the moor[2]," Martha replied enthusiastically. "Do you like it?"

"No," Mary said coldly.

"The moor will vary with the seasons. You'll like it in the spring and summer. There will be beautiful flowers and birds. The air will be so fresh to breathe. I can't imagine living elsewhere," declared Martha.

---

2 moor [mʊr] (n.) 沼澤地
3 chores [tʃɔːrz] (n.) (pl.) 家庭雜務
4 bathe [beɪð] (v.) 幫⋯⋯洗澡

 "You are a strange servant," Mary declared. She gradually became annoyed. "In India, we didn't talk to servants. We gave orders. Anyway, are you my servant?"

"Well, I work for Mrs. Medlock and assist in household chores[3] and stuff. However, I'll be responsible for cleaning your room and bringing you food."

"Who's going to dress me, then?"

"You aren't capable of dressing yourself?" Martha sounded surprised.

"In India, my servant used to dress me and bathe[4] me too. I remember them doing both tasks with efficiency."

✓ *Check Up* *Choose the correct answer.*

_____ 1. Martha didn't enjoy living close to the moor.   (True) (False)

"I am afraid you'll have to dress yourself," Martha declined. "My mom always says we ought to take care of ourselves, no matter how important we are."

While Martha kept on quoting[5] her mother's words, Mary felt a mixture of frustration[6] and anger. Martha's words destroyed her expectation of a life similar to that in India.

She began crying uncontrollably, "You don't know anything! It's different in India!" Mary had a chip on her shoulder[7] about not being treated like a princess.

🎧15 "Oh, miss, please stop crying. I never intended to slight[8] you. No offense. Yes, it's my fault. I don't know anything. I don't qualify as an efficient maid."

Martha felt guilty of fueling[9] Mary's outburst[10].

Mary stopped crying shortly because Martha sounded fairly kind. Martha switched[11] the topic of their conversation to stories about her family. Martha said she worked on meager[12] wages here because the country's overall economy was worsening.

✓Check Up *Choose the correct answer.*

_____ 2. Martha is responsible for _____ .
  Ⓐ dressing Mary
  Ⓑ providing domestic service
  Ⓒ taking care of consumers

5 quote [kwoʊt] (v.) 引述
6 frustration [frʌ'streɪʃən] (n.) 挫折
7 have a chip on one's shoulder 某人產生好鬥的情緒
8 slight [slaɪt] (v.) 輕視；怠慢
9 fuel ['fju:əl] (v.) 刺激
10 outburst ['aʊtbɜ:rst] (n.) 情緒爆發
11 switch [swɪtʃ] (v.) 轉換；更改
12 meager ['mi:gər] (a.) 不足的

Owing to the recession[13], she didn't have an adequate selection of jobs, and she needed to provide some money to her family.

Martha also said she had a brother named Dickon. He liked to ride his horse on the moor and play with other animals. Mary was instantly interested in hearing this, because she always wanted her own animal.

"Will Dickon play with me?" Mary asked.

"Well, you might see him around if you're lucky. I think you should learn to play by yourself, miss. There are plenty of gardens around the house to play in except one. That one is locked, and you can't get into it."

"Why?"

"Well, ten years ago, Mrs. Craven fell down from a tree in the garden. Unfortunately, she died, at the peak[14] of her youth. Since then, Mr. Craven locked the garden and buried the key."

Mrs. Craven

Mary was intrigued[15] by the idea of a secret garden. Just then Mary and Martha heard a bell ringing.

Martha stopped cleaning and said, "It's Mrs. Medlock. She's ringing for me. Now, you go out and play. The fresh air will do you good."

Mary went out and explored the gardens. She passed by a particular garden with walls around it, but it seemed to have no door to enter.

Right then a robin[16] attracted her attention. Up in a tree, the robin was singing to her. The friendly chirping[17] of the robin made her smile.

 Choose the correct answer.

_____ 3. Mrs. Carven died from an illness.　　　(True) (False)

13　recession [rɪˈseʃən] (n.) 經濟衰退
14　peak [piːk] (n.) 巔峰
15　intrigue [ɪnˈtriːg] (v.) 被……激起好奇心
16　robin [ˈrɑːbɪn] (n.) 知更鳥
17　chirp [tʃɜːrp] (v.) 發啁啾聲

🎧18 She also noticed a gardener digging the soil. The gardener seemed bad-tempered and in an irritable[18] mood. Still, she went over to see what he was doing.

"What's your name?" she asked the gardener.

"Ben Weatherstaff," declared the tough gardener.

At the moment, the robin flew onto the gardener's shoulder and sang to him. The gardener smiled, and he didn't look crabby[19] anymore.

"I don't have any friend here. He is my only friend," said Ben.

"I don't have any friend, either," said Mary.

Meanwhile, the robin jumped up and down and sang to Mary. The gardener concluded, "I think he wants to be your friend."

The robin chirped a while and flew into the secret garden. "Look! He flew into the garden with no door! I wonder how I could get into the garden."

Ben stopped smiling and warned, "Mr. Craven imposed[20] a restriction on the entry to this garden. No one is allowed without Mr. Craven's permission. Now, excuse me, I have to carry on working."

Ben left without saying goodbye.

---

18 irritable [ˈɪrɪtəbəl] (a.) 易怒的;急躁的
19 crabby [ˈkræbi] (a.) 易怒的
20 impose [ɪmˈpoʊz] (v.) 強加

🎧19   That night, just as Mary thought about how she could get into the secret garden, she heard a strange noise.

At first, she thought it was the wind. Then she suspected it couldn't be the wind because it came from inside the house. It sounded like a boy wailing[21].

The next day Mary asked Mrs. Medlock if she had heard a boy crying. Mrs. Medlock looked surprised at first; however, she dismissed[22] Mary's inquiry by telling her it was nothing.

She also told Mary to stop thinking about nonsense in the depths of the night. Surely, Mary was not convinced[23] of Mrs. Medlock's answer. She was keen on uncovering the mystery by herself.

✓ *Check Up* *Choose the correct answer.*

_____ 4. Mary believed the origin of the noise was _____.
     A the wind
     B the pub nearby
     C a boy

_____ 5. Mary was not persuaded by Mrs. Medlock's   (True) (False)
     explanation about what she had heard in the middle
     of the night.

21   wail [weɪl] (v.) 嗚咽
22   dismiss [dɪsˈmɪs] (v.) 把……打發走
23   convince [kənˈvɪns] (v.) 使信服

3 The Secret Garden

One day, when Mary was roaming[1] the gardens as usual, the robin flew by to accompany[2] her.

"Hey, robin! Do you like the weather today? The strong wind and heavy clouds are already gone. I guess spring is coming!"

---

1 roam [roʊm] (v.) 漫步；漫遊
2 accompany [əˈkʌmpəni] (v.) 陪伴

🎧21 The robin sang and hopped[3] along as Mary walked. Mary began to pursue[4] the robin by hopping like him. Just as they were having fun hopping, the robin stopped at a place.

The place looked like a hole.

Mary took a close observation[5] of the hole. From an angle, her perfect vision told her there was something in the hole.

She bent down on her knees and started excavating[6] the earth. She found an old key.

"Perhaps this was the key to the secret garden," she thought.

3 hop [hɑːp] (v.) 齊足跳
4 pursue [pərˈsuː] (v.) 追趕
5 observation [ˌɑːbzərˈveʃən] (n.) 觀察
6 excavate [ˈekskəveɪt] (v.) 挖掘

🎧22 The next day Martha came by to give Mary a gift.

"My mom got you a gift, Mary. It's a jump rope!" Martha exclaimed.

"Your mom?"

"Yes, I told Mother all about you yesterday. Mom said with a great deal of emphasis[7] that you'd love to have a new jump rope. She went out and bought it from a rope manufacturer[8]."

In India, Mary was accustomed[9] to showing great resistance to people's kindness. However, while in Yorkshire, her habitual tension[10] with people had vanished[11].

✔Check Up *Choose the correct answer.*

____ 1. Mary found the old key in a _____.
　　Ⓐ hole
　　Ⓑ mine
　　Ⓒ technical laboratory

7　emphasis ['emfəsɪs] (n.) 強調
8　manufacturer [,mænjʊ'fæktʃər] (n.) 工廠
9　accustom [ə'kʌstəm] (v.) 使習慣於……
10　tension ['tenʃən] (n.) 緊張
11　vanish ['vænɪʃ] (v.) 消失

What was the reason she had changed?

Perhaps, it was Martha's kindness, love, and care that had disarmed[12] her hostility[13] and selfishness.

Mary was touched by the behavior of Martha's mom. Mary didn't know what to say about such voluntary kindness, for she had never received a gift since her birth. Her very first gift was a jump rope. It was of great significance.

Mary looked at her gift and asked, "What's a jump rope?"

"Well, let me show you how to use it," answered Martha.

She then taught Mary the fundamental[14] steps of how to skip with the new jump rope. Mary thought it was easy and fun. With the jump rope, she could play by herself.

"Thank you, Martha," said Mary. "It's such a valuable gift for me. I know your family doesn't have much money. I really owe[15] you a lot."

---

12 disarm [dɪs'ɑːrm] (v.) 緩和
13 hostility [hɑː'stɪlɪti] (n.) 敵意
14 fundamental [ˌfʌndə'mentl] (a.) 基礎的
15 owe [oʊ] (v.) 欠

That was the first time Mary had ever expressed recognition[16] of someone's benevolence[17].

Martha was glad Mary liked the gift. She smiled and said, "Now, go and have fun with it."

Mary skipped[18] her way to the secret garden and found the robin there.

√ *Check Up* *Choose the correct answer.*

_____ 2. Mary received a _____ from Martha's mother.
    Ⓐ present
    Ⓑ crown
    Ⓒ jumper

16 recognition [ˌrekəgˈnɪʃən] (n.) 認可
17 benevolence [bɪˈnevələns] (n.) 善意
18 skip [skɪp] (v.) 蹦蹦跳跳

🎧25 Mary said to the robin, "Thanks to you, I found the key to the secret garden. Could you show me the door today?"

The robin hopped onto some old climbing ivy[19] on the wall. Then somehow the ivy was blown aside by the wind. There was a gap[20] in the layers[21] of ivy. Mary saw a rusty knob[22] that had previously been hidden by the ivy. Was it a part of the door?

Mary took out the key from her pocket. She unlocked and slowly pushed open the big heavy door. Mary couldn't believe her eyes. It was so marvelous! After 10 years, the garden was finally opened for the first time.

✔ Check Up

3. What happened that led to Mary's discovery of the door to the secret garden?

_____

19 ivy ['aɪvi] (n.) 常春藤
20 gap [gæp] (n.) 缺口；裂口
21 layer ['leɪər] (n.) 層
22 knob [nɑːb] (n.) 球形把手

It was a wonderful garden. Although it looked deserted in comparison with other gardens, there were rose trees everywhere. The garden's high walls were dominated[23] by roses, too.

On the ground, there were many wild flowers. Mary looked closely at the plants and found green little shoots. She was excited to find there was still life in the garden.

So, to give the budding[24] shoots more light and air, Mary began clearing away the weeds. As she worked, she began to have this secret wish to restore[25] the garden.

---

23 dominate ['dɑːmɪneɪt] (v.) 支配；控制
24 budding ['bʌdɪŋ] (a.) 萌芽的
25 restore [rɪ'stɔːr] (v.) 恢復

🎧 27 When Mary returned to her room for lunch, Martha was there setting up the table.

"Martha, I have a request for you. Could you help me get a spade[26] and some seeds? I was intrigued by Ben's work."

"Sure. Dickon can help you get a spade and some seeds. Being engaged[27] in gardening and watching the plants grow is lots of fun," replied Martha.

Mary mentally calculated[28] her savings. "My allowance[29] from Mrs. Medlock should be sufficient, and I can afford them. Would you ask Dickon to buy them for me?"

"Absolutely! I will ask him to bring them to you."

"And I will be glad to meet him."

---

26 spade [speɪd] (n.) 鏟子
27 engaged [ɪnˈgeɪdʒd] (a.) 忙於……的
28 calculate [ˈkælkjʊleɪt] (v.) 計算
29 allowance [əˈlaʊəns] (n.) 零用錢

28 Martha took a good look at Mary. What a dramatic[30] change to Mary's personality!

When Mary first came here, she was selfish and bad-tempered. However, she was now sensitive[31] and treated everyone in a polite and friendly fashion. She connected to people around her, too.

Martha was sure when Dickon and Mary met each other, they would become good friends.

Check Up *Choose the correct answer.*

_____ 4. What did Mary think she needed for gardening?
    Ⓐ Electronic devices.
    Ⓑ Seeds and soil.
    Ⓒ Seeds and a spade.

_____ 5. Mary got a loan to cover the expenses for gardening. (True) (False)

30 dramatic [drə'mætɪk] (a.) 戲劇性的
31 sensitive ['sɛnsɪtɪv] (a.) 敏感的

4 Getting to Know Dickon

For a week, Mary spent most of her time working in the secret garden. She was content to see new shoots coming out each day.

"Soon there will be flowers everywhere," she predicted[1] complacently[2].

One day, on her way to the secret garden, she heard some pleasant music. The sweet melody really appealed[3] to her.

---

1 predict [prɪˈdɪkt] (v.) 預報；預言
2 complacently [kəmˈpleɪsəntlɪ] (adv.) 滿足地
3 appeal [əˈpiːl] (v.) 有吸引力

It came from a boy under a tree, who was playing on a wooden pipe. He was surrounded by squirrels, robins, and rabbits. It looked as if these creatures were listening to the music.

Initially[4], Mary thought she should withdraw[5]. However, the music was so beautiful that she decided to stay. So, she stood aside and remained silent.

Suddenly, the boy stopped playing. He looked at Mary and said, "Animals don't like it when you move abruptly[6]. Their interpretation[7] of an abrupt move is some kind of threat. You were right when you stood still."

🎧 **31** Mary was pleased to hear that compliment.

"Hi, I'm Dickon. You must be Mary. I got you a spade and some seeds."

"Thanks, Dickon." Mary knew the boy was Dickon before he introduced himself.

Like Martha, he had the same characteristic[8] of speaking with enthusiasm[9]. Mary liked Dickon right away, for he seemed like a friendly and moral person.

"I can help you plant these seeds. Where's your garden?"

Check Up Choose the correct answer.

_____ 1. Mary decided not to leave because _____.
　　Ⓐ she liked the music
　　Ⓑ she wanted to know the theme of the music
　　Ⓒ leaving without saying goodbye was not proper

4　initially [ɪ'nɪʃəli] (adv.) 起初
5　withdraw [wɪð'drɔ:] (v.) 離開；移開
6　abruptly [ə'brʌptli] (adv.) 突然地
7　interpretation [ɪn,tɜ:rprɪ'teɪʃən] (n.) 解釋
8　characteristic [,kerɪktə'rɪstɪk] (n.) 特色；特性
9　enthusiasm [ɪn'θu:ziæzəm] (n.) 熱心；熱情

That question made Mary redden[10] with embarrassment[11]. She was too embarrassed to say anything about the secret garden.

Besides, involving Dickon in her secret undertaking[12] worried her a little. However, she thought maybe she could trust Dickon.

"Would you keep a secret?" Mary took a deep breath as she looked around to make sure nobody was near. "If you disclose[13] this secret, I'll be in big trouble."

"Don't worry. I'm good at keeping secrets. I keep many secrets for the animals here."

His comment provided her with some relief, and so Mary said, "I found a secret garden. No one wants it. There are many flowers, but they need to be taken care of."

"Where is it?" Dickon got curious.

"Follow me, but promise me not to tell anyone."

"Deal."

---

10 redden ['rɛdn] (v.) 臉紅
11 embarrassment [ɪm'bærəsmənt] (n.) 窘
12 undertaking ['ʌndərteɪkɪŋ] (n.) 工作
13 disclose [dɪs'kloʊz] (v.) 透露

Mary led Dickon into the secret garden, and they spent all day planting and weeding. Mary thought she had the best fun ever.

Dickon really knew how to combine work with pleasure. Besides, Dickon was a gifted gardener. He taught Mary some useful agricultural[14] knowledge such as the importance of proper distribution of the seeds on the soil.

At the end of the day, Dickon promised not only to keep the secret but also to help Mary take care of the garden.

"I can come here to help you every day," Dickon assured her gladly. "This garden needs to be further weeded[15]."

Mary was thrilled[16] to have Dickon as one of her good friends in Yorkshire.

 Choose the correct answer.

_____ 2. Dickon was unable to help Mary every day, and his help would be temporary. (True) (False)

---

14 agricultural [ˈægrɪˌkʌltʃərəl] (a.) 農業的
15 weed [wiːd] (v.) 除草
16 thrilled [θrɪld] (a.) 非常興奮的

🎧 34   When Mary returned home, she told Martha all about her encounter with Dickon.

"I also have something to tell you, Mary. Mr. Craven wants to see you tonight because he is leaving tomorrow for a few months."

"Oh, that's nice," said Mary, though she must be very careful not to let Mr. Craven find out about her work in the secret garden.

After dinner, Mrs. Medlock took Mary to Mr. Craven's room. Mr. Craven was a hunchbacked[17] man with black hair and a sad face. When Mary entered the room, Mr. Craven was smoking a cigarette.

"How are you, child?" Mr. Craven spoke in a solemn[18] mode.

"I'm . . . well." Mary sounded a bit nervous.

"What do you usually do in this quiet and rural[19] neighborhood?"

"I play outside with my jump rope. I also enjoy watching plants grow and talking to the robin."

Mr. Craven looked kindly at Mary and said, "Is there anything you want before I leave?"

---

17 hunchbacked ['hʌntʃbækt] (a.) 駝背的
18 solemn ['sɑːləm] (a.) 嚴肅的；莊重的
19 rural ['rʊrəl] (a.) 鄉村的

Mary was excited about Mr. Craven's kind offer. She bravely seized the chance to tell her uncle she needed a garden to plant.

"There are plenty of gardens here, and they are all very lovely. How I wish I had my own garden to plant beautiful flowers."

✓ *Check Up* *Choose the correct answer.*

_____ 3. Mr. Craven had an unusual _____.
  A back
  B chest
  C gene

🎧36 Mr. Craven's initial response to Mary's request was surprise. Then he smiled a little and took a good look at the girl. "I used to know someone like you. She loved gardens as much as you do."

Mr. Craven looked as if he was reminiscing[20] the good old times.

"Of course you can have a garden," Mr. Craven said approvingly. "You can pick any garden you want."

"Thank you, Uncle!" Mary grinned[21].

"All right, I must go to bed now. I'm leaving very early tomorrow."

Mary never thought she could acquire[22] her uncle's approval[23] to have her own garden. Mary was so happy. On the way back to her room, she hopped and skipped like a happy little robin.

 Check Up *Choose the correct answer.*

_____ 4. Mary secured her uncle's go-ahead to possess one of his gardens.

True
False

20 reminisce [ˌrɛmɪˈnɪs] (v.) 追憶；回想
21 grin [grɪn] (v.) 露齒而笑
22 acquire [əˈkwaɪr] (v.) 獲得
23 approval [əˈpruːvəl] (n.) 批准；認可

44

5 The Crying Sound at Night

One night Mary woke up from her dream, for she heard the crying sound again. This time she was determined to find out who it was. She traced the crying sound down the corridor[1] and arrived in a spacious[2] room.

The room looked like an art gallery[3], because its walls were hung with paintings. These artistic creations were mostly representations of seemingly important figures.

✓ *Check Up* *Choose the correct answer.*

_____ 1. Which of the following words best explains the definition of the word "spacious" in the previous paragraph?
    Ⓐ Spacey.   Ⓑ Roomy.   Ⓒ Spatial.

---

1 corridor [ˈkɔːrɪdər] (n.) 走廊
2 spacious [ˈspeɪʃəs] (a.) 寬敞的
3 gallery [ˈgælərɪ] (n.) 畫廊;美術館

As Mary went further inside, she saw a little boy with a tearful pale face on a bed. He seemed to be in absolute shock.

"Are you a ghost?" asked the boy fearfully.

"No, I'm Mary Lennox. Who are you?"

"I'm Colin, Colin Craven. My father owns this house."

"Oh, then, you're my cousin. I didn't know Uncle Craven had a son." Mary sounded surprised.

"No one told me you lived here," noted Colin.

"Well, it's a long story. Anyway, why are you crying?"

"I am dying, you see. I have a very strange disease. The doctor says even if I do live, I will grow up as a hunchback just like my father."

"Does your father see you often?"

"No, he doesn't want to see me. Seeing me would remind him of my dead mother. My mother died soon after I was born."

39 "My parents died, too," said Mary. "That's why I'm here."

"Do you like it here?"

"Yes, I especially enjoy myself in my garden."

As soon as she said it, Mary realized she just confided[4] something secret.

"Your garden? Which one?" Colin was curious.

✓ *Check Up* *Choose the correct answer.*

_____ 2. Colin thought he saw a _____ when Mary appeared in his room.

Ⓐ tenant   Ⓑ ghost   Ⓒ shadow

4 confide [kənˈfaɪd] (v.) 透露；吐露

"Oh . . . uh . . . It's just a garden around here," Mary stuttered[5].

"Tell me which one it is. I want to know the location," Colin insisted.

"Uh . . . That's really not important."

"If you don't tell me now, I'll summon[6] the servants to make you. They all listen to me when my father is away."

"Please . . . don't do that. All right, I'll tell you, but, would you keep a secret?"

"I guess I would, but I never had a secret."

Mary told Colin all about the secret garden. Colin's eyes widened as Mary mentioned about the robin, the key, and Dickon.

She also accounted[7] how the secret garden was getting increasingly beautiful under her care and with Dickon's help. She also praised Dickon's knowledge of agriculture.

5　stutter ['stʌtər] (v.) 結結巴巴地説話
6　summon ['sʌmən] (v.) 召來
7　account [ə'kaunt] (v.) 説明

 "Maybe, you should come to the secret garden with us," Mary urged[8]. "I can ask Dickon to push you in your wheelchair[9]. I think the fresh air will do you good."

"Fresh air," said Colin slowly, as he looked out of the window. "I think I'd like that."

That night Mary also gave Colin a detailed account about her life in India. Colin was really amused by Mary's description, and he began to smile and cheer up.

Colin liked Mary very much and wanted Mary to visit him every day. Before they said good night, Mary promised to visit him again tomorrow.

Check Up Choose the correct answer.

_____ 3. Mary had no alternative but to reveal her secret about the secret garden because of Colin's _____.
    A warning   B crying   C complaint

8 urge [ɜːrdʒ] (v.) 慫恿
9 wheelchair ['wiːltʃer] (n.) 輪椅

🎧42 After that night, Mary's visit became constant[10]. Colin didn't tell anyone about Mary's visits, and neither did Mary. Normally, the two children would share stories and also have a session[11] of extensive[12] reading.

They enjoyed contemporary literature and invested quite some time in putting their literary[13] ideas in writing. Their dislikes were religious and scientific reading materials.

One day while they were having a great time together, the door opened suddenly. It was Mrs. Medlock with a panel[14] of Colin's doctors. They looked at each other with surprise.

"Oh, Lord, what's going on here?" asked Mrs. Medlock.

"It's none of your business," Colin spoke like the master of the house. "I invited Mary. I want her to keep me company."

---

10 constant ['kɑːnstənt] (a.) 固定的
11 session ['seʃən] (n.) 活動時間
12 extensive [ɪk'stensɪv] (a.) 廣泛的
13 literary ['lɪtəreri] (a.) 文學的
14 panel ['pænl] (n.) 小組

"But, sir, this girl might give you the flu," said Mrs. Medlock.

"Just look at me. I feel much better when she's around. It's entirely acceptable for her to be here."

"But . . . sir . . ."

"Enough! You heard what I said. Now, leave us."

Mrs. Medlock apologized to the doctors when they left Colin's room.

However, one of the doctors told Mrs. Medlock that they had to agree with Colin. "It's a rare phenomenon[15]," said the doctor. "The boy is really looking a lot healthier."

✔Check Up *Choose the correct answer.*

_____ 4. Mrs. Medlock was worried about _____.
    Ⓐ Colin's symptoms
    Ⓑ Colin getting some kind of infection, such as a flu
    Ⓒ the doctors' qualification

15 phenomenon [fɪˈnɑːmɪnɑːn] (n.) 現象

6 Colin's Rage

🎧 44 Mary visited Colin every day. The rain poured for a whole week, and she couldn't go to the secret garden.

One morning when it was perfectly sunny outside, she went straight to the secret garden.

Dickon was there, and he was busy gardening. After a week of rain, there were already plenty of flowers giving a beautiful display of red, yellow, pink, and orange. The flowers were simply remarkable!

✓ Check Up Choose the correct answer.

_____ 1. There was a week's absence of gardening because
_____.

    Ⓐ Mary and Dickon abandoned the secret garden
    Ⓑ it rained for a week
    Ⓒ Dickon resisted going to the secret garden

Mary and Dickon worked in the secret garden all day. When Mary came back to her room in the evening, she saw Martha rushing nervously into her room.

"Mary! You have to help us with this emergency[1]. Colin likes you, but he accused[2] you of not visiting him. Now, he's crying and yelling in protest against your defiance[3] of him."

"I was busy. How can he be so selfish? We should put a stop to his tendency[4] toward such an abuse[5] of privilege."

When Mary and Martha arrived in Colin's room, Mrs. Medlock and a crew[6] of servants were there trying to appease[7] him. Mary moved forward to speak to Colin.

"What's wrong with you?" Mary asked.

"Oh, my back aches so badly. Where were you today?"

"I went out with Dickon."

"Stop going out with him." Colin cast a jealous look at Mary. "You come see me every day."

1 emergency [ɪˈmɜːrdʒənsi] (n.) 緊急情況；突然事件
2 accuse [əˈkjuːz] (v.) 指控；控告
3 defiance [dɪˈfaɪəns] (n.) 藐視
4 tendency [ˈtɛndənsi] (n.) 傾向
5 abuse [əˈbjuːs] (n.) 濫用
6 crew [kruː] (n.) 一夥人
7 appease [əˈpiːz] (v.) 平息；緩和

"Nonsense! I am not your maid. You can't make me come here every day."

"I'll make the servants bring you down here."

"Fine! Then I won't talk to you. No one can make me talk."

Upon hearing Mary's retort[8], Colin started to scream with frenzy[9]. "Oh, my back hurts! I am dying!"

"Stop! Stop screaming!" Mary shouted at the top of her lungs.

✓*Check Up* *Choose the correct answer.*

____ 2. As soon as Mary entered Colin's room, they had a _____.
  Ⓐ dispute   Ⓑ negotiation   Ⓒ delicious meal

8 retort [rɪ'tɔːrt] (n.) 回嘴；反駁
9 frenzy ['frenzi] (n.) 發狂

🎧 47 Colin stopped, for no one, including Mrs. Medlock or even his father, had ever shouted at him. Mrs. Medlock and Martha shifted[10] their attention to Mary and stood in awe[11] of her outburst. Nevertheless, Colin sobbed quietly to himself.

"You are so spoiled, Colin. Your back is absolutely fine," said Mary. "Martha, give me a hand. Let me look at his back."

Mary was determined to secure a lasting settlement[12] of Colin's fear. Mary examined Colin's back very closely.

"Essentially[13], your back is as straight as anyone else's," said Mary, after a critical[14] examination of Colin's back. "There's nothing wrong, nothing at all."

Mary believed that Colin's illness was only in his mind and he would be OK if only he made up his mind to be.

"Really? Are you sure?"

Mary's words were a startling[15] contrast to what Colin had always heard from people around him.

---

10 shift [ʃɪft] (v.) 轉換；轉移
11 awe [ɔː] (n.) 畏怯
12 settlement ['setlmənt] (n.) 解決
13 essentially [ɪ'senʃəli] (adv.) 實質上；本來
14 critical ['krɪtɪkəl] (a.) 仔細的
15 startling ['stɑːrtlɪŋ] (a.) 令人吃驚的

🎧48 For such a long time, Colin had always been told that either his back would become as crooked as his father's or he was sick and would die young.

Now, Mary's assuring words made him realize maybe he wasn't sick. Maybe it was just fear that made him sick. Besides, when Mary was with him, he did feel much stronger. Mary's company made him less fearful.

"Maybe you're right. Maybe I'm not sick. I guess my fear of death got the best of me."

"That's right. I think you need to go out, use your muscles a bit, and breathe some fresh air," Mary recommended.

✓ Check Up *Choose the correct answer.*

3. What was Colin's actual reason for his fear of death or fear of his back becoming crooked?

_____

_____ 4. What made Colin confused about his health?
Ⓐ Fear of death.
Ⓑ Fear of undergoing a plastic surgery.
Ⓒ Fear of darkness.

However, Mrs. Medlock was opposed to what Mary had said, and she expressed her immediate concern to Colin, "Don't listen to her, sir. There is no way you can go out like this. Besides, you can't walk."

"Silence!" Colin shouted. "I want to go out with Mary, no matter what. Besides, I have a wheelchair, don't I?"

Mary moved forward and whispered to Colin, "Dickon will be pleased to push you in your wheelchair. We'll take you to the secret garden. You won't believe how beautiful it is now."

Colin laughed, and so did Mary. Now, they both looked forward to the outing.

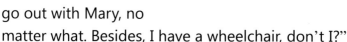

✓ Check Up *Choose the correct answer.*

_____ 5. What could be inferred from the previous passage above?
    Ⓐ Dickon would be awarded a suitable sum of money for pushing Colin in his wheelchair.
    Ⓑ The people enjoying the secret garden would consist of Colin, Mary, and Dickon.
    Ⓒ Colin would defend any of Dickon's suggestions.

7 The Determined Colin

The next day Colin was ready to go out. He gave orders to Mrs. Medlock that no one should follow. When Colin was taken to the doorstep, Mary and Dickon were there waiting for him.

Collin wanted to believe his health was OK. Still, he wasn't so sure about the outdoors. He looked a little nervous as if he were chained to the wheelchair.

To overcome his fear, Colin took a deep breath and said, "Let's go, shall we?"

On their way to the secret garden, Colin didn't speak, for everything around him seemed so strange yet exciting to him.

Soon he heard Mary say, "Here's the entrance. Now, Colin, close your eyes. Don't open them until I tell you to do so."

Colin followed Mary's instructions[1] dutifully[2].

Colin knew he was being pushed into the secret garden. When Mary told him to open his eyes, he looked around the garden with a bright smile.

There were so many flowers in vivid colors, and there were also birds and butterflies here and there.

Colin was amazed to see a garden with such life and vitality[3]. He really loved the atmosphere of the garden. It was the first time for him to experience such a beautiful and tranquil[4] place.

As the sun shone on Colin's face, he realized that he felt different.

"I'll get better!" Colin hollered[5]. "I know I will, and I'll live forever and ever."

1 instruction [ɪnˈstrʌkʃən] (n.) 指示
2 dutifully [ˈduːtɪfəli] (adv.) 忠實地
3 vitality [vaɪˈtælɪti] (n.) 生氣；活力
4 tranquil [ˈtræŋkwɪl] (a.) 平靜的；安靜的
5 holler [ˈhɑːlər] (v.) 大叫

Dickon kept pushing Colin around the garden as Mary recounted[6] how the secret garden went from a lifeless territory[7] to a lively place.

Colin was curious about everything, and he asked the names of the entire unknown plants. Learning the names was so educational for him.

"I want to come here every afternoon," Colin exclaimed. "It'll be fun to watch these flowers and trees grow."

"Maybe you can help us tend the garden," said Dickon light-heartedly. "We'd love to see expansion of the gardening team membership. I'm sure sooner or later you'll be strong enough to walk."

✔ *Check Up* *Choose the correct answer.*

_____ 1. Colin closed his eyes in preparation for entering the secret garden. (True) (False)

_____ 2. Which of the following best estimates the frequency of Colin's future visits to the secret garden?
Ⓐ An average of 3 days a week.
Ⓑ Four days a week with Sundays included.
Ⓒ Every day.

6 recount [rɪ'kaʊnt] (v.) 詳述
7 territory ['terɪtɔːri] (n.) 領土
8 improvement [ɪm'pruːvmənt] (n.) 增進；改善
9 feeble ['fiːbəl] (a.) 衰弱的；無力的
10 resolution [ˌrezə'luːʃən] (n.) 決心

"Do you really think I'll be able to . . . walk?" Colin asked.

"Definitely!" Mary cheered on. "You look much better now. With your rate of improvement[8], I believe you'll be able to walk very soon."

"That's right, Colin!" Dickon exclaimed. "We can help you practice!"

That day Colin committed himself to undertaking a solid yet reasonable plan to learn to walk. He called the plan his health experiment.

In the beginning, his steps were feeble[9]. Colin trembled, but he demonstrated his resolution[10] to learn.

🎧55 Mary and Dickon
saw Colin's exhibition[11]
of his resolution in his
unceasing efforts. In fact,
Colin's dedication to the
promotion of his health
touched both of them
so much that they also
resolved[12] to offer their
assistance to Colin.

Mary and Dickon's
original sympathy
for Colin's physical
inability turned to strong
determination to help Colin recover his full potential[13].

Meanwhile, in implementing[14] Colin's recovery plan, the three children quickly formed bonds[15] of friendship.

Every day throughout the next several weeks, Colin challenged his limits by practicing hard. The practice was often laborious, but Colin never displayed signs of giving up.

11 exhibition [ˌeksɪˈbɪʃən] (n.) 展現
12 resolve [rɪˈzɑːlv] (v.) 決心
13 potential [pəˈtenʃəl] (n.) 潛能
14 implement [ˈɪmplɪment] (v.) 實施；執行
15 bond [bɑːnd] (n.) 聯結

57 Soon he could finish walking around the garden by himself. He didn't need to rely[16] on Dickon's assistance any more.

Colin's input of time and effort had turned out to be worthwhile. However, he was not satisfied. Once he could walk properly, he started to learn to run.

The intensive practice expanded his vital capacity, and he could easily cope with[17] the challenge of running now. With little output of effort, he could run as fast as Mary. The net[18] result of Colin's hard work really amazed Mary and Dickon.

Check Up Choose the correct answer.

_____ 3. It could be inferred that the children hoped the best outcome of Colin's walking practice should be _____.

[A] that Colin could at least walk dependent on a cane
[B] that Collin would be independent from his father
[C] that Colin could walk like everyone else

16 rely [rɪ'laɪ] (v.) 依賴；信賴
17 cope with 應付；處理
18 net [nɛt] (a.) 最終的；淨值的

"My next goal is to outrun[19] Dickon. Let's hold a championship footrace. We will compete, and the competition will make each of us stronger. If I get to be the champion, it would be a great achievement for all of us because you both have helped me a lot. And the goal after that is to cycle around the garden with a bicycle," claimed Colin ambitiously.

"You look quite competitive now, and I know you have great potential," said Dickon. "Still, I think your speed will never compete with mine. But if you should win first place in the race, I would ask my mom to present you with a certificate[20]. How's that?"

Dickon's criticism[21] wasn't an apparent attempt to hurt Colin. After spending the past several weeks together, Mary, Colin, and Dickon had become very good friends.

All three children laughed. They knew it wasn't Dickon's intention to be a critic of Colin's abilities. He was simply trying to tease Colin.

Up until now, no one knew Colin could walk except Mary and Dickon. It was Colin's idea to keep it a secret. Colin always asked Dickon to push him in the wheelchair when they went home.

One day, when the kids were relaxing in the secret garden, Mary asked Colin, "Don't you want your father to know that you are well now?"

"I'll let him know, but I want it to be a big surprise," said Colin. "I want to surprise him when he comes home."

Mary agreed. She and Colin were really looking forward to Mr. Craven's return.

✓ *Check Up* *Choose the correct answer.*

_____ 4. It was Colin's expectation to _____.
  Ⓐ ride a bicycle with an electric motor that could help him go faster than Dickon
  Ⓑ run faster than Dickon
  Ⓒ be an inventor

_____ 5. No one knew Colin could walk with the exception of Mary, Dickon and Mrs. Medlock. ⓉTrue ⒻFalse

19　outrun [aʊtˈrʌn] (v.) 跑得比……快
20　certificate [sərˈtɪfɪkət] (n.) 證書
21　criticism [ˈkrɪtɪsɪzəm] (n.) 批評

8 Mr. Craven's Big Surprise

🎧59 The secret garden and the children came alive that spring. However, there was a man who didn't feel alive. His name was Archibald Craven, Collin's father.

For the past ten years, he had traveled to many beautiful places in Europe. He traveled because he was trying hard to forget the sadness back home.

He tried and tried to find some happiness, but instead, he felt more melancholic[1]. His inner soul was bitter and miserable.

One day he came by a beautiful stream in Austria. He looked at the water, flowers, and trees around him. It was so serene[2] and quiet.

As he was appreciating the beauty in front of him, he felt asleep and began to dream. In the dream, he heard the voice of his dead wife.

"Archie! Archie!"

---

1 melancholic [ˌmɛlənˈkɑːlɪk] (a.) 憂鬱的
2 serene [sɪˈriːn] (a.) 安詳的

"My dear!" Mr. Craven shouted in his dream. "Where are you?"

"In the garden," replied the voice.

Mr. Craven woke up as the dream ended. He thought to himself, "In the garden? But the door is locked. Besides, the key is buried."

Mr. Craven looked at the stream and the beautiful flowers around him again. The beauty before his eyes reminded him of the secret garden. Then he began to think of Colin.

"What a bad father I am," he said to himself. For so many years, Mr. Craven had almost completely ignored[3] Colin's existence[4].

---

3 ignore [ɪgˈnɔːr] (v.) 忽視
4 existence [ɪgˈzɪstəns] (n.) 存在

He could not bear to look at his son because Colin painfully reminded him of his late[5] wife. He only saw Colin when Colin was asleep.

"I miss Colin." Mr. Craven wept. "I will go home to see Colin now. Perhaps I should interpret[6] this dream as a signal[7] for me to go home."

When Mr. Craven arrived home, he found a confused Mrs. Medlock.

"Collin isn't like his normal self, sir," said Mrs. Medlock. "He looks better now, and he spends a lot of time during the day outside. Mary and Martha's brother, Dickon, push him around in his wheelchair, and we are not allowed to come near them. I am so worried, sir. His appetite has become extremely large, and it fluctuates[8] sharply. Sometimes he doesn't eat, but sometimes he eats more than a healthy boy does. He's in the garden now."

"In the garden." That was the phrase[9] he had heard from his dead wife in the dream.

He rushed out of the house and toward the garden he had never set foot in for ten years. He found the door closed and heard wild laughing and the shouting of children inside. As he stood there listening, the door swung open. Then a healthy boy with average height ran out and straight into his arms.

"Uh, who . . . who are you?" asked Mr. Craven.

"It's me, Father. I'm Colin. Don't you recognize me?"

"But . . . you look so different."

"Yes, Father. I can't believe it myself, either. It was like magic. The garden, Mary, and Dickon all contributed[10] to my wellness. You see, Father, I'm going to live forever and ever. Aren't you happy?"

✓ *Check Up* *Choose the correct answer.*

_____ 1. Mr. Craven heard his dead wife's voice in _____.
     A hell   B the background   C his dream

_____ 2. Mr. Craven couldn't distinguish Colin from Dickon.   True False

---

5 late [leɪt] (a.) 去世的;已故的
6 interpret [ɪnˈtɜːrprɪt] (v.) 作解釋
7 signal [ˈsɪɡnəl] (n.) 信號
8 fluctuate [ˈflʌtʃueɪt] (v.) 變動
9 phrase [freɪz] (n.) 說法
10 contribute [kənˈtrɪbjuːt] (v.) 貢獻

Mr. Craven embraced his son tightly in his arms and cried. On the one hand, he felt sorry for his previous indifference[11]. On the other hand, he was profoundly happy for Colin.

He was speechless for a moment, but shortly he managed to retain his composure[12].

He said to Colin, "Let's go into the garden, Colin, and you can tell me all about the magic."

Inside the garden there were blossomy roses, towering trees, and chirping robins. The children shared their stories and interesting anecdotes[13] with Mr. Craven.

---

11 indifference [ɪnˈdɪfərəns] (n.) 漠不關心；冷淡
12 composure [kəmˈpoʊʒər] (n.) 沉著；平靜
13 anecdote [ˈænɪkdoʊt] (n.) 軼事；趣聞

He laughed and cried at times, but most of the time he beheld the unfamiliar but sweet face of his adorable[14] son.

He simply couldn't believe the healthy Colin in front of him was once so ill. For the first time in ten years, he had a feeling of release.

At dusk, as Mary, Dickon, Colin, and Mr. Craven walked back to the house, the servants gathered at the porch[15] to greet them.

Mrs. Medlock, Martha, and other servants had the greatest surprise in their lives and rubbed their eyes constantly. The wheelchair that Dickon pushed was empty, and their little master had a straight back and walked with firm steps.

What's more, their master of the house, Mr. Craven, had the brightest smile on his face.

In tears, Mrs. Medlock said to Martha, "He's back! He's really back! That's the gentleman I knew ten years ago."

Check Up Choose the correct answer.

3. When Mrs. Medlock said, "That's the gentleman I knew ten years ago," what did she imply?

_____

14 adorable [əˈdɔːrəbəl] (a.) 可愛的
15 porch [pɔːrtʃ] (n.) 門廊

EXERCISES

A Multiple Choice.

_____ ➊ Mary's mother was a/an _____ before she died.
   a) scholar in the academic field
   b) beautiful woman only interested in going to parties
   c) author

_____ ➋ Mary's parents died _____.
   a) of a disease
   b) in a bloody battle
   c) of an armed murder

_____ ➌ Mr. Craven was a/an _____.
   a) rich man
   b) editor of a publication company
   c) producer of many films

_____ ➍ Martha worked as a maid in the Cravens' residence because _____.
   a) the country was in the middle of inflation
   b) it was a penalty imposed by the governor of Yorkshire
   c) she was helping to improve her family's financial situation

_____ ➎ Which of the following statements best describes Yorkshire?
   a) An urban area with a string of outbreaks of violence and sexual harassment.
   b) An industrial area with lots of construction and engineering projects and is polluted by acid rain.
   c) A rural area with grassy plains.

_____ ❻ Which of the following identities best describes Ben Weather staff's job?
a) An assembly representative for Yorkshire.
b) A gardener.
c) A seasoned pilot.

_____ ❼ How did Mary find the key to the secret garden?
a) She found the key attached to the door of the secret garden.
b) She found the key hidden in an opening in the wall behind a picture frame.
c) The robin led her to a hole in the ground.

_____ ❽ Which of the following statements is true about Dickon?
a) He was a healthy boy who developed friendship with Mary.
b) He was Colin's brother.
c) Like Colin, he was entitled to half of Mr. Craven's possessions.

_____ ❾ Mary met Mr. Craven before he left on a trip. He was planning to be away for a few months. The meeting took place _____.
a) at a coal mine
b) in Mr. Craven's room
c) at a photography institute

_____ ❿ What did Mary usually hear in the middle of the night?
a) Noise from workers constructing a house.
b) A boy crying.
c) People shouting during a congressional meeting.

_____ ⑪ Colin was Mary's _____.
a) cousin whom she had never met before
b) nephew
c) investor

_____ ⑫ Colin was angry one day because Mary didn't visit him. Mary failed to visit Colin because _____.
a) she was being monitored and her visit was restricted
b) she went out with Martha
c) she was busy in the secret garden the whole day

_____ ⑬ What was Mary's suggestion for Colin to deal with his illness?
a) Colin should boost his protein intake.
b) Colin should get some mental therapy and take alternative medicine.
c) Colin should go out and use his muscles a bit.

_____ ⑭ In the secret garden, Colin _____.
a) learned to walk
b) learned to sing
c) was bound to his wheelchair all the time

_____ ⑮ What was the most unlikely reason that brought Mr. Craven back from his trip?
a) He missed Colin.
b) He needed to attend an important convention in Yorkshire.
c) He dreamed about his wife.

B Fill in the Blanks.

relocate	treat	constant
jump rope	dress	

❶ In India, Mary wasn't capable of _____ herself; her servant always helped her put on her clothes.

❷ After Mary's parents died, she was _____ to her uncle's house in Yorkshire.

❸ Mrs. Medlock was in charge of the Cravens' residence because Mr. Craven was _____ away.

❹ Although a _____ was cheap, Mary thought it was a valuable gift from Martha.

❺ Mary was accustomed to _____ her servants rudely.

C Complete the following excerpts using the correct form of the words provided.

by	with	in	out

Mary went 1)_____ of the house and explored the gardens. She passed 2)_____a particular garden 3)_____ walls around it, but it seemed to have no door to enter. Right then a robin attracted her attention. Up 4)_____ a tree, the robin was singing to her.

elsewhere   breathe   moor   vary

The 5)_____ will 6)_____ with the seasons. You'll like it in the spring and summer. There will be beautiful flowers and birds. The air will be so fresh to 7)_____. I can't imagine living 8)_____.

resolution   unceasing   undertake
solid   demonstrate

That day Colin committed himself to 9)_____ a 10)_____ yet reasonable plan to learn to walk. He called the plan his health experiment. In the beginning, his steps were feeble. Colin trembled, but he 11)_____ his resolution to learn. Mary and Dickon saw Colin's exhibition of his 12)_____ in his 13)_____ efforts.

D Rewrite the order of words provided.

❶ at/Mary/and/still/if/the/looked/plants/alive/were/closely/wondered/they

Mary _____

_____

❷ years/to/in/ten/he/places/many/the/For/Europe/traveled/past/beautiful/had

For _____

_____

E Complete the following sentences using the correct form of the words provided.

demand	endorse	claim
recount	put forth	

❶ The professor _____ the cultural and historical background of ancient Greek philosophy.

❷ The economist _____ his positive estimates for next year's economy after carefully analyzing many trends in the global market.

❸ The Republic of Ireland's Ministry of National Defense signed the letter that _____ the withdrawal of British troops.

❹ Yesterday the President _____ the new law that has changed out national pension plan.

❺ The government _____ that the worker's so-called revolution constituted a criminal act.

作者介紹

1849，Frances Hodgson Burnett 出生於英國的曼徹斯特。1865 年，父親過世之後，全家便遷移到美國。

母親於 1870 去世後，她一度認為自己可以以寫作為生，因為她一直熱愛寫作，當時她開始在雜誌上發表言情小說。

她的作品廣受歡迎，但一直到 1886 年出版了第一本兒童文學作品《Little Lord Fauntleroy》後，她的文學聲譽才建立起來。

她接下來的作品包括了《秘密花園》（1888）和《小公主》（1909），這也是她至今最為人所知的作品。她曾結過兩次婚，於 1905 年入籍美國，卒於 1924 年。

角色介紹

瑪麗・雷諾克斯	出生於印度，年紀九歲大，在投靠姑丈之前，脾氣一直很壞。
卡瑪拉	瑪麗在印度時的女僕，因為瑪麗的父母很忙，所以由她負責照顧瑪麗。
亞齊伯・克雷文	瑪麗的姑丈，被說成是「悽慘而駝背的人」，因為他的愛妻早逝，他就四處旅行，很少去看看他的兒子柯林。
柯林	克雷文先生的兒子，他一直認為自己會變成駝背，而且不會活得很久。
梅德洛管家	克雷文先生家的管家，自從柯林的母親去逝之後，就由她負責照顧柯林。
瑪莎	克雷文先生家的一位女僕，也是迪肯的姐姐。
班・威勒史達	一位老園丁，負責照料克雷文家的花園。
迪肯	瑪莎的弟弟，與住在沼澤地上的動物們相處愉快。

故事提要

瑪麗‧雷諾克斯是一位壞脾氣又自私的小女孩，在她九歲時，父母雙雙亡於一場疫疾，於是她便被帶英國，投靠約克郡的姑丈。但儘管她住在姑丈家，卻少有機會見到姑丈。

一開始，她很不喜歡約克郡，然而在一群朋友和動物的友好對待下，她開始接觸這裡的每一個人。然而她卻發現到，在姑丈家裡頭，似乎有著許多悲傷的秘密。

首先，那裡有一座秘密花園，自從姑姑過世之後，那座花園就被荒廢了。然後，屋子裡還有一個臥病在床的小男孩，應該就是她的表弟。後來，在她的悉心照料下，秘密花園改變了風貌，而表弟也變得健康了。

最後，當克雷文結束歐洲一趟長時間的旅行返家後，他更發現了一個新的秘密，然而這一次，這個秘密卻出奇地令人欣喜。

I 前往約克郡

pp. 6-7 瑪麗‧雷諾克斯出生於印度。她今年九歲，留著一頭稀疏的黃髮，臉蛋清瘦，總是擺著一副臭臉。

她不像一般人那樣能常常和家人在一起，她的父親出任英國官職，在印度擁有大筆財產。因為父親從事政治，工作繁重，瑪麗很少見到父親。她的父親是一個典型的英國官員——事業第一，家庭第二。

瑪麗的母親風采迷人，個性開放，她不太照顧女兒，只對做頭髮或是參加宴會有興趣。

因此瑪麗則被交給印度僕人卡瑪拉去照顧。

事實上呢，瑪麗也跟她父母親一樣，這一家子的人都只關心自己的事情。

瑪麗為所欲為，總是對卡瑪拉頤指氣使。身為僕人的卡瑪拉，也只能順任著這位大小姐予取予求。

pp. 8-9 某天酷熱的早晨，瑪麗發現平日替她準備早餐的卡瑪拉，換成了另一位僕人。

「你在這裡做什麼？叫卡瑪拉來！」瑪麗憤怒地對僕人吼叫。

「我很抱歉，雷諾克斯小姐，卡瑪拉不會來了。」僕人驚慌地答道。

「我恨死她了！要是讓我看到她，我一定要狠狠踢她一腳！」瑪麗語帶威脅說著。

不久，瑪麗看見母親帶著一名男子來到花園，他們兩個大人並沒有發現瑪麗就在旁邊。

瑪麗偷聽了他們的對話，知道鎮上正流行著瘟疫，人們死的死，逃的逃，她還聽到卡瑪拉也染病而死。

一聽到這裡，瑪麗感到非常害怕，她有時會一個人偷偷地哭，或是用睡覺來讓自己逃避事實。然而，恐懼依舊如影隨形。

pp. 10-11 這一天，瑪麗醒來後，發現整間房子靜悄悄的，身旁一個僕人都沒有，接著她聽見大廳傳來幾個男子的聲音：

「雷諾克斯家的遭遇實在令人遺憾，只能說運氣太差了。」其中一位男子說著。

「他們家還有一個小孩，我們都沒見著她。這個可憐的孩子現在在哪？」另一人問。

這時瑪麗突然打開房門，出來和他們見面。他們起初嚇了一跳，但隨即對瑪麗表達同情之意：

「可憐的女孩，你爸媽染病去世，你家的僕人也都跑光了。」

瑪麗並不想念父母，因為她和父母並沒有很親，此刻她只關心自己的事。「那我要住在哪裡？」她問道。

瑪麗沒有像一般孤兒一樣被送往慈善機構，而是被告知將會被帶回英國，去和姑丈亞齊伯・克雷文一起住。克雷文是約克郡當地有頭有臉的家族。

瑪麗從來沒聽過這位姑丈的事，也不曉得自己在英格蘭有親戚，更不知道約克郡這個地方在哪裡。她只希望姑丈會是個好人，能讓她為所欲為。

pp. 13 瑪麗帶著成堆的行李來到英國，管家梅德洛來到港口接她。年長的梅管家生性保守拘謹，信仰虔誠。

梅管家氣色紅潤，黑色的眼珠炯炯有神；她說話的語調，讓瑪麗聯想到父親的一位朋友，那個人是澳洲聯邦法庭的法官。

瑪麗不喜歡這位管家，而梅管家也不怎麼喜歡她。

「你是我的傭人嗎？」瑪麗問。

pp. 14-15 「你最好注意一下你的態度。」梅管家冷冷地答道：「我只替克雷文先生工作。我負責克雷文家的內務，而當克雷文先生外出時，我就身兼他的代理人。無論如何，我是來帶你去約克郡的。所以動作快點！我們要趕兩點的火車。」

在車上，瑪麗靜靜看著窗外的景色。梅管家雖然對瑪麗沒有好印象，覺得她需要管教管教，但她還是開了口：

「你姑丈的家在約克郡的邊界，那是一座很大的老莊園，莊園裡頭有大約一百間房間，不過大部分都上了鎖。房子外面有各式各色的花園，還有雕工精細的梁柱。你喜歡這些嗎？」

「我沒興趣。」瑪麗不屑一顧。

「你真是個個性古怪的小孩。不過也無妨，雖然克雷文先生要負責你在約克郡的生活費用，但他未必需要關心你。大部分的時間他都待在房裡，不和他人往來，甚至不出門投票。一個駝背、擁有萬貫家財的人，直到他結婚那天，我才見到他笑。」

pp. 16 「他結婚了嗎？」瑪麗有點驚訝。

「他結過婚。克雷文太太十年前去世了。」

「她去世了？」瑪麗開始感到好奇。

「是的。之後克雷文先生就對事物麻木了。他把自己關在房間，與外人隔絕，當然他也不會想看到你，所以你最好遵守規則乖乖聽話。」

這班直達車雖然不用轉車，但這趟火車行程足足花了將近一天的時間。當火車抵達約克郡時，天已經黑了。這是一個冷風颼颼的夜晚，和印度的夜晚十分不同。

2 在莊園的冒險

pp. 17 當瑪麗跟著梅管家回到克雷文先生的莊園時，兩人都累壞了。隨即瑪麗便被帶到她的房間，房裡已經升起暖暖的爐火，桌子上還準備好了食物。

「這就是你的房間。」梅管家說：「吃過晚餐後就上床睡覺，不要在屋子裡蹓躂。如果你想要住在這邊，就請你遵守規矩。」

pp. 18-19 隔天瑪麗醒來，看到一位年輕女僕在幫忙整理房間。女僕身材瘦，雙頰紅潤。

「你是誰？」

「我是瑪莎，小姐。」女僕神色怡然地回答。

瑪麗從窗簾向外望去，只見到一片遼闊的草地，看不到什麼樹或房子。她問瑪莎：

「那邊是什麼？」

「那是溼地。」瑪莎興奮地說著。「你喜歡溼地嗎？」

「不喜歡。」瑪麗冷漠地說。

「溼地會隨著季節變化。春天和夏天會有美麗的花朵和鳥兒，空氣也很新鮮，你一定會喜歡的。真無法想像還有別的地方會像這裡一樣適合居住。」瑪莎說。

「你這女僕真奇怪。」瑪麗表示。她漸漸感到一陣煩躁。「我在印度生活的時候，從來不跟僕人說話的。我們只下命令。對了，你是我的僕人嗎？」

「這個嘛，我替梅管家做事，協助她處理克雷文家的各種雜務。我是被指派要替小姐清掃房間和準備食物的。」

「那誰要負責幫我換衣服？」

「你不會自己穿衣服嗎？」瑪莎驚訝地問。

「我在印度的僕人會幫我穿衣服、洗澡，她們的動作都很俐落。」

pp. 20-21 「很抱歉，但你得自己穿衣服。」瑪莎拒絕道：「我媽媽一直教導我，無論我們的身分為何，都必須學會自己照顧自己。」

瑪莎繼續講述著母親的金玉良言，這讓瑪麗感到惱怒。瑪莎所說的，讓她的期待成空，她無法過著像在印度時的生活了。

她不禁大哭了起來：「你什麼都不懂！在印度時根本不是這樣的。」瑪麗很生氣，她覺得自己沒有像小公主一樣被人侍候，感到很委屈。

「哦，小姐，請你別哭了。我不是要怠慢你，也沒有惡意。是，這都是我的錯，我不了解狀況，我是無能的僕人。」

看到瑪麗哭，瑪莎感到非常內疚。

聽到瑪莎這樣好聲好氣的一番話，瑪麗一下子就不哭了。瑪莎換了個話題，聊起了自己的家庭。瑪莎說，她之所以來這裡賺這麼一點微薄的薪水，是因為整個國家的經濟都不景氣。

pp. 22-23 因為經濟蕭條的關係，沒有什麼工作機會可以選擇，但總是要出來為家裡賺點錢。

瑪莎還提到了自己的弟弟迪肯。迪肯喜歡騎著馬在溼地上蹓躂，和其他動物一起玩耍。聽到這裡，瑪麗立刻有了興致，因為她一直以來就希望能養隻動物。

「迪肯會喜歡跟我一起玩嗎？」瑪麗問瑪莎。

「如果有緣的話，你可能會見到他。小姐，你可以學著幫自己找點樂子啊。這裡有很多花園可以去玩，不過那邊那座花園上了鎖，不能進去。」

「為什麼？」

「這是因為啊，在十年前，克雷文太太從那座花園的一棵樹上摔了下來，不幸過世，當時她還很年輕呢。就是從那時候開始，克雷文先生就把花園鎖上，還把鑰匙埋起來。」

瑪麗對這座「秘密花園」產生了興趣。就在此時，傳了來一聲鈴聲。

瑪莎停下手邊的工作，對瑪麗說：「是梅管家，她有事要找我。小姐，你可以出去外面走走。去呼吸一下新鮮的空氣，對你有好處的。」

於是瑪麗來到外面，四處逛起了花園。她來到一座很特別的花園，花園四周都圍著牆，卻找不到門可以進去。

這時，一隻知更鳥吸引了她的注意。知更鳥站在樹梢上，向她啼唱，友善的啁啾聲，讓她露出了笑容。

pp. 25 她注意到了旁邊還有一位正在挖土的園丁，園丁看起來脾氣不怎麼好，一副不好惹的樣子，不過瑪麗還是走向他，想看他在做什麼。

「你叫什麼名字？」瑪麗問園丁。

「班．威勒史達。」體格粗壯的園丁回答。

就在這時，那隻知更鳥飛到了園丁的肩膀上，對他啾啾叫。園丁露出了笑容，看起來沒那麼不好惹了。

「我在這裡沒有朋友，牠是我唯一的朋友。」班說。

「我也沒有什麼朋友。」瑪麗回答。

就在此時，知更鳥雀躍地跳上跳下，對瑪麗啼叫。園丁於是說道：「我想牠想跟你做朋友。」

知更鳥啁啾了一會兒後，便飛回秘密花園。

「你看！牠飛進去那座沒有門的花園裡了。不知道我要怎樣才能進去。」

班收起笑容，對瑪麗提出警告說：「克雷文先生禁止任何人進入那座花園。沒有克雷文先生的允許，誰都不能去。很抱歉，我要繼續工作了。」

班沒說再見便離開了。

pp. 26 當天夜裡，正當瑪麗想著如何潛入秘密花園時，她聽見了奇怪的聲響。

起初她以為是風聲，但後來覺得不可能是風，因為怪聲是從屋子裡傳來的，而且聽起來像是小男孩的哭聲。

隔天，瑪麗問梅管家有沒有聽見男孩的哭泣聲，梅管家一開始露出驚訝的表情，但隨即就表示什麼都沒聽到。

她還告誡瑪麗，不要半夜一個人胡思亂想。當然，她的回答是無法打發瑪麗的，她要自己去解開這個謎題。

3 揭開秘密花園的面紗

pp. 27 這一天，瑪麗在花園中散步，知更鳥飛到了她身旁來和她作伴。

「哈囉，知更鳥，今天的天氣很好吧。沒有刮強風，也看不到烏雲了，我想春天要來了吧！」

pp. 28-29 知更鳥一邊唱著歌，一邊雀躍地跟著瑪麗，瑪麗也跟著知更鳥蹦蹦跳跳。兩個一路上蹦蹦跳跳地玩著，最後知更鳥在某處停了下來──一個看似洞穴的地方。

瑪麗仔細觀察洞穴，從某個角度望去，她清楚看見洞裡有東西。

於是她蹲下來，開始挖開洞旁的泥土，結果發現了一把老舊的鑰匙。

「搞不好這就是通往秘密花園的鑰匙。」瑪麗心中暗想。

隔天瑪莎帶了個禮物給瑪麗。

「瑪麗小姐，我媽媽要送你一個禮物。是跳繩喔！」瑪莎興奮地說。

「你媽媽送的？」

「是啊，我昨天和媽媽提起你的事情，我媽媽就說你一定會想要一條新的跳繩。這是她跟一家做繩子的公司買來的。」

過去在印度的時候，瑪麗對他人的善意毫不領情，但是來到約克郡之後，她和他人的關係就不再緊繃了。

<u>pp. 30-31</u> 到底是什麼改變了她？

也許是因為瑪莎的善良、愛心和呵護，瓦解了她的敵意和自私的態度。

瑪莎母親的舉動，讓瑪麗十分感動。對於別人這種主動的善意，她不知道該如何回應，因為這是她生平第一次收到禮物。這一副跳繩，是她收到的第一份禮物，這對她可是意義重大。

瑪麗看著這份禮物，問道：「什麼是跳繩？」

「這個嘛，我來教你怎麼用吧。」瑪莎答道。

瑪莎從基本的步驟開始，教導瑪麗如何使用這副新跳繩。瑪麗覺得跳繩既簡單又有趣，而且可以自己一個人玩。

「謝謝你，瑪莎，這份禮物很珍貴。我知道你們家沒有什麼錢，真的很謝謝你們。」瑪麗說。

這是瑪麗第一次對別人的善意有所表示。

瑪莎很高興瑪麗喜歡這份禮物，她笑道：「現在就去好好玩吧。」

瑪麗興沖沖地來到秘密花園，看到了知更鳥。

<u>pp. 32</u> 瑪麗告訴知更鳥：「都是你的功勞，我找到了秘密花園的鑰匙。你今天能告訴我入口在哪裡嗎？」

知更鳥跳到爬滿長春藤的老舊圍牆上，此時一陣風吹開了一片長春藤，在層層藤蔓中露出了一條縫隙。瑪麗看到長春藤裡頭藏了一個生鏽的把手，那就是門的把手嗎？

瑪麗從口袋中拿出鑰匙，打開了門鎖，緩慢地推開沉重的大門。眼前的景色令人驚奇，瑪麗簡直不敢相信自己的眼睛。十年來，秘密花園第一次被開啟了！

<u>pp. 34-35</u> 這是一座美麗的花園。雖然和別的花園比起來，它顯得有些荒廢，但園內到處都是玫瑰樹，連高聳的圍牆上也爬滿了玫瑰花。

草皮上開出了各色各樣的野生花朵。瑪麗仔細盯著植物瞧，還看到了新抽的綠芽，她興奮地發現這座花園依舊生生不息。

為了讓幼芽能得到更多的陽光與空氣，瑪麗開始動手拔雜草。此時，一個念頭悄悄浮上心頭：她想重新修復這座花園。

當瑪麗午餐時間回到房間時，瑪莎正在擺設餐具。

「瑪莎，我有一個要求。你可以幫我找一把鏟子和一些種子嗎？我也想試試班的工作。」

「沒問題，迪肯可以幫你找來鏟子和種子。做園藝很有趣喔，可以看到植物如何生長。」瑪莎回答。

　　瑪麗暗自盤算身上的錢。她說：「梅管家給我的零用錢，應該夠買那些東西吧。你可以叫迪肯幫我買嗎？」

　　「當然好啊！我會叫他買好後送來給你。」

　　「我也很想看看他呢。」

pp. 36 瑪莎看著瑪麗，驚訝她的個性轉變如此之大。

　　記得瑪麗剛來的時候，個性自私，脾氣又壞，但現在，她變得心思細膩，而且待人和善有禮，和身邊的人也都有所互動。

　　瑪莎相信，迪肯和瑪麗一定很快就會變成好朋友了。

4　新朋友迪肯

pp. 37 接下來的一個星期，瑪麗大都待在秘密花園裡。每天都能看到不同的新芽抽出，她感到很滿足。

　　「很快這裡就會開滿了花。」她滿意地預言。

　　這一天，在前往秘密花園的途中，傳來了一陣悅耳的音樂，瑪麗深深地被吸引住。

pp. 38-39 音樂是從大樹下傳來的，那裡有一位男孩正吹奏著木笛。男孩身邊圍繞著松鼠、知更鳥和兔子，牠們似乎也很享受音樂。

　　一開始，瑪麗想避開，但因為笛聲實在太美妙，所以還是佇足下來，靜靜地站在一旁聆聽。

　　忽然，男孩停止吹奏，他看著瑪麗，開口道：「動物會怕人們突如而來的舉動，對牠們來說，那是一種威脅。像你剛剛那樣站著，就對了。」

　　瑪麗聽到他這番話，感到很開心。

　　「你好，我是迪肯。你就是瑪麗吧。我幫你帶來了鏟子和一些種子。」

　　「謝謝你，迪肯。」瑪麗早就猜出迪肯的身分。

　　迪肯跟瑪莎一樣，說話的語氣都很熱情。迪肯的人看起來友善又正直，瑪麗馬上就對他產生好感。

　　「我可以幫你種這些種子。花園在哪邊？」

pp. 40-41 這個問題問得瑪麗臉都紅了，她覺得很窘，不知怎麼提秘密花園的事情。

　　此外，要讓迪肯一起參與花園的秘密工作，她也感到有點不安。不過，她想自己應該能信任迪肯的。

　　「你願意保守這個秘密嗎？」瑪麗深吸一口氣，看看四周，確定沒有人聽見：「如果你洩漏了這個秘密，那我的麻煩就大了。」

　　「別擔心，我很能守秘密的。我替這裡很多的動物保密呢。」

　　迪肯的話讓瑪麗安心不少，於是瑪麗說道：「我找到一座秘密花園，那裡被荒廢了。園裡開滿了很多花，需要照料。」

　　「那座花園在哪裡？」迪肯很好奇。

　　「跟我來，不過你不可以告訴別人喔。」

　　「沒問題！」

　　瑪麗帶著迪肯來到秘密花園，兩個人花了一整天的時間播種和除草，瑪麗從沒有玩得那麼盡興過。

迪肯很懂得將娛樂寓於工作之中，此外，他還是個很有天分的園藝高手。他教了瑪麗一些很好用的農業知識，像是如何將種子平均播灑在土壤上。

這一天結束時，迪肯向瑪麗保證，他非但不會洩漏秘密，還會幫忙照顧花園。

「我可以每天來這裡幫忙。」迪肯樂於承諾道，「這座花園還需要除去更多的雜草。」

瑪麗非常興奮，她很高興能在約克郡結交到迪肯這個好朋友。

pp. 42 -43 當晚瑪麗回到屋內，她告訴瑪莎今天和迪肯碰面的點點滴滴。

「我也有事情要告訴你，瑪麗。克雷文先生晚上想要見你，因為他明天一早就要出門，要幾個月後才會回來。」

「好。」瑪麗回答。她必須要謹慎一點，不能讓克雷文先生發現她到秘密花園的事。

用完晚餐後，梅管家帶著瑪麗來到克雷文先生的房間。克雷文先生是個黑髮的駝背男子，看來一臉哀傷。瑪麗進到房間時，克雷文先生正抽著雪茄。

「你還好嗎，孩子？」克雷文先生以嚴肅的口吻詢問。

「嗯……我……我很好。」瑪麗有些緊張。

「在這個安靜的鄉下，你都做些什麼？」

「我會到外面去玩跳繩。我也喜歡觀察植物的生長，和知更鳥說說話。」

克雷文先生和藹可親地看著瑪麗，問她：「在我出門之前，你有想要什麼東西嗎？」

瑪麗對克雷文先生親切的提議感到很開心，她便趁機大膽地告訴姑丈，說她想要有個花園，可以種種東西。

「這裡有很多漂亮的花園，我也想要有一個自己親手種的花園，可以種很多漂亮的花卉。」

pp. 44 克雷文先生起初對瑪麗的要求感到有點詫異，不過他隨即笑了笑，看著這位小女孩。「我以前認識一個人，她像你一樣很喜歡花園。」

克雷文先生露出一副像是在緬懷往日美好時光的樣子。

「當然囉，你可以有一座自己的花園，你就自己去選一座吧。」克雷文先生一口答應。

「謝謝你，姑丈。」瑪麗笑道。

「那好，我現在得上床睡覺了，我明天一大早就要出門。」

瑪麗作夢也沒想到，姑丈會答應自己的請求，讓她可以擁有自己的花園。她感到非常地開心。她就像一隻快樂的知更鳥一樣，蹦蹦跳跳地回到房間。

5 夜半的啜泣聲

pp. 45 一天夜裡，瑪麗從夢中甦醒，她又聽見了上次的哭聲。她決定這次一定要找出到底是誰在哭泣。她尋著哭聲，沿著走廊走去，來到了一間寬敞的房間。

那個房間看起來有點像美術館，牆上掛了很多畫，那些肖像畫上的人物似乎都是很重要的人士。

pp. 46 -47 瑪麗往房裡走去，看到床上躺著一個臉色蒼白、滿臉淚水的小男孩，而男孩正用震驚的表情望著她。

「你是鬼嗎？」小男孩害怕地問。

「不是，我叫瑪麗．雷諾克斯。你是誰？」

「我是柯林‧克雷文。我爸爸是這座莊園的主人。」

「喔，那你是我的表兄弟囉。我不知道克雷文姑丈有小孩。」瑪麗很驚訝。

「沒有人跟我說你住進來了。」柯林説。

「這個説來話長。對了，你為什麼在哭？」

「你看，因為我快死了。我得了一種奇怪的病。醫生説，就算我活下來，也會像我爸爸一樣變成駝背。」

「你爸爸有常來看你嗎？」

「沒有，他不想看到我，因為他看到我，就會想到我去世的媽媽。我媽媽在我出生不久後，就死去了。」

「我爸媽也都死掉了。」瑪麗説，「所以我才會到這裡來。」

「那你喜歡這裡嗎？」

「喜歡啊！特別是當我去我的花園的時候。」

話一出口，瑪麗才想到自己正洩露了秘密。

「你的花園？哪一座花園啊？」柯林好奇地問著。

pp. 48-49 「嗯……這個嘛……就是在這裡的一座花園啦。」瑪麗開始結巴。

「告訴我是哪一座，我想要知道位置在哪裡。」柯林追問。

「嗯……這又不重要。」

「如果你不告訴我，我會叫僕人逼你説出來。我爸不在，他們都得聽我的。」

「拜託，不要這樣。好吧，我告訴你，但是你要保守秘密。」

「好，我應該可以答應你，只是我從來就沒有過秘密。」

瑪麗將秘密花園的事情告訴了柯林，包括知更鳥和迪肯的事，柯林睜大眼睛聽得入神。

她説，在自己和迪肯的悉心照顧下，秘密花園現在變得越來越漂亮了。她還説迪肯很懂農藝。

「你應該跟我們一起去秘密花園。我可以請迪肯推輪椅帶你去，那裡的空氣很新鮮，對身體很好。」瑪麗慫恿著。

「新鮮空氣。」柯林緩慢地重複著這幾個字，望向窗外：「我想我會喜歡的。」

當晚，瑪麗還跟柯林聊到她過去在印度的生活，柯林聽著瑪麗的描述，覺得很有趣，開始笑了起來，變得精神奕奕。

柯林很喜歡瑪麗，希望她每天都能來找自己玩。在互道晚安之前，瑪麗答應明天會再過來找他。

pp. 50 此後，瑪麗便常常去找柯林。而他們彼此都沒有跟任何人説起這件事。通常，兩個人會説説自己的事，也會一起看看書。

他們喜歡現代文學，寫作時會花很多時間去鋪陳他們的文學點子。他們最不喜歡看的是宗教和科學的書。

這一天，就在兩個人玩得開心時，房門忽然被打開，那是梅管家和柯林的醫師群。大家驚訝地看著彼此，對現場的情況感到十分意外。

「天啊，這是怎麼一回事？」梅管家吃驚地問。

「不要你管。」柯林用主子的語氣説道：「是我邀請瑪麗來的，我希望她來陪我。」

pp. 52「但是少爺,這個女孩可能會把流行病毒傳染給你啊。」梅管家説。

「你看看我!自從瑪麗來了之後,我整個人感覺好多了。她在這裡根本不會有問題。」

「但是少爺……」

「夠了!你聽到我説的了——現在,馬上出去!」

梅管家一邊向醫師道歉,一邊趕緊離開房間。

不過有位醫師説,他們不得不認同柯林的話,他告訴梅管家:「這可真罕見了,少爺看起來的確健康多了。」

6 憤怒的柯林

pp. 53 現在瑪麗每天都會去看柯林。不過這一個星期以來,外面下著傾盆大雨,使得瑪麗沒辦法去秘密花園。

這一天早上,外面才放晴,瑪麗便直奔秘密花園而去。

瑪麗在園內看到了迪肯,他正在整理花園。經過了一個星期的雨水滋潤,長出了好多花朵,一片色彩繽紛,形成一幅壯麗的花海景象。

pp. 54-55 瑪莉和迪肯整天都在花園裡工作,當她傍晚返回房間時,她看到瑪莎神色慌張地衝進來。

「瑪麗,你得幫幫我,出事了!柯林很喜歡你,可是他怪你今天沒去看他。他現在大哭大鬧,抗議你看不起他。」

「我今天都在忙耶,他怎麼可以那麼自私呢?我們要讓他改一改,不能這麼愛擺姿態。」

瑪麗跟著瑪莎來到柯林的房間,梅管家和底下的一群僕人正試著安撫柯林。瑪麗走向前去和柯林説話。

「你是怎麼了?」瑪麗問。

「我的背一直在痛,你今天去哪裡了?」

「我和迪肯在一起。」

「不准你再跟他出去。」柯林看著瑪麗,眼神充滿忌妒,「你每天都要來這裡找我。」

「什麼跟什麼!我又不是你的女僕。你不能規定我每天都要來。」

「我會叫僕人每天都把你帶過來。」

「好啊!那我不會跟你講話,我看你要怎麼辦。」

聽到瑪麗這樣回嘴,柯林開始抓狂尖叫,大喊:「我的背好痛,我快死了!」

「停!停止!不要再叫了!」瑪麗使勁喊道。

pp. 56-57 柯林停止了尖叫,過去無論是梅管家,甚至是他父親,都沒有人大聲命令他過。梅管家和瑪莎看到瑪麗發了這麼大的脾氣,兩個人都嚇到了。不過柯林倒是乖乖聽話,只見他小聲地啜泣著。

「柯林,你被大家寵壞了。你的背根本沒問題嘛。」瑪麗説:「瑪莎,幫我一下,我要看一下柯林的背。」

瑪麗想要徹底解決柯林的恐懼,她仔細檢查著柯林的背部。

「基本上,你的背很直,就跟一般人一樣。」瑪麗在詳細診視後開口道:「你的背沒事,一點問題也沒有。」

瑪麗認為,柯林的病來自心理,只要他堅定信心,就能夠不藥而癒。

「真的,你確定嗎?」

瑪麗這番話,和他以前聽到的,完全不一樣。

長久以來，大家都説，他要嘛就像他父親一樣會駝背，要嘛很年輕就病死。

現在瑪麗這種信誓旦旦的説法，讓柯林了解到自己可能根本就沒有生病，搞不好這病都是被自己嚇出來的，況且當他和瑪麗在一起時，就覺得自己好多了。只要有瑪麗在旁邊，他就比較不怕了。

「也許你説的對，我根本就沒生病。我想我只是因為怕死，才怕出病來的。」

「沒錯，你應該多出去走走的。多用用你的肌肉，呼吸些新鮮空氣。」瑪麗提出建議。

pp. 58 不過，梅管家似乎很不認同瑪麗的話，她擔心地立刻説道：「少爺，別聽她的，你不可以隨便出去啊。何況，你沒辦法自己走路呀。」

「別吵！」柯林大喊，「我一定要跟瑪麗到外面去。再説，我有輪椅不是嗎？」

瑪麗傾身向前，在柯林耳邊説著悄悄話：「迪肯很樂意幫你推輪椅喔。我們帶你到秘密花園去，你一定不敢相信現在那裡有多漂亮。」

柯林和瑪麗兩人笑了出來，他們對這次的出遊充滿期待。

7　柯林的決心

pp. 59 隔天，柯林已經準備好要出門，他還命令梅管家，讓誰都不准跟來。他們把柯林推到門口時，瑪麗和迪肯已經在那裡等候他了。

柯林寧願相信自己的身體很健康，只不過他不是很有把握，自己可以走出戶外。他的神情看起來有點緊張，整個人好像被綁在輪椅上似的。

為了克服自己的恐懼，他深深吸了一口氣，説道：「我們該出發了吧？」

pp. 60-61 在前往秘密花園的路上，對柯林來説，周遭的一切都是那麼新奇，讓他驚訝得説不出話來。

不久，他聽到瑪麗説：「這裡就是入口。柯林，來，閉上你的眼睛，我説睜開眼睛，你才可以睜開喔。」

柯林安份地遵從瑪麗的命令。

柯林感到自己正被推進秘密花園，當瑪麗要他睜開眼睛後，他露出燦爛的笑容，四處張望著。

這裡有這麼多爭妍鬥豔的花，而且到處都有小鳥和蝴蝶。

看到花園裡生機盎然的景象，柯林感到很驚奇。他真的很喜歡這裡的感覺，他第一次來到這麼美麗靜謐的地方。

陽光灑落在他的臉上，他知道這一切的感覺是如此不同。

「我一定會好起來的！」他喊道：「一定會的！我會活得很久很久！」

pp. 62-63 迪肯推著柯林在花園裡逛，瑪麗跟在旁邊，説起原本荒廢的秘密花園，是如何變得生氣勃勃的。

柯林看到什麼都覺得好奇，花園裡所有植物對他都是陌生的，他一一問起它們的名字。光是得知這些植物的名稱，就讓他好好上了一課。

「以後我每天下午都要來！」柯林嚷嚷道：「看這些花草樹木長大，一定很有趣。」

「也許你可以幫我們整理花園。」迪肯愉悅地說道:「我們很高興秘密花園能加入新的成員,我想你不久就可以站起來走路了。」

「真的嗎?你覺得我可以……站起來走路嗎?」柯林問道。

「一定可以的!」瑪麗替他加油打氣:「你現在看來已經好很多了,照這種速度下去,你一定很快就可以站起來走路了。」

「沒錯,柯林!」迪肯喊道:「我們還可以幫助你練習走路!」

那天,柯林就開始了他紮實但適量的「學走路計畫」,他把這項計畫稱作「健康實驗」。

剛開始時,他的雙腳站不太住,全身都在顫抖,但他拿出了自己的決心,要好好學走路。

pp. 64-65 瑪麗和迪肯目睹了柯林的堅毅,看到他不停地努力嘗試,以及為健康所做的努力,都讓兩個人很感動,決定要好好助他一臂之力。

他們原本是同情柯林身體上的障礙,但現在他們把同情心轉變成一種強烈的決心,決定要幫助柯林完全康復起來。

而就在柯林的康復計畫進行的同時,這三個小孩也很快就建立起了堅韌的友誼。

接下來的幾個星期,柯林在艱困的練習下,每一天都有一點進展。這些練習往往很辛苦,但他毫不退縮。

很快地,他就能自己繞完花園一圈。他再也不需要倚賴迪肯的幫忙了。

柯林所花費的時間和心血,顯得有所代價。然而,他並不滿足於此,等到他能正常走路之後,他還想學習跑步呢。

這些緊密的練習,讓他的肺活量變大,現在,學習跑步對他來說不是什麼難事了。他只要稍微努力跑一下,就可以跑得和瑪麗一樣快了。柯林努力後的最終成果,讓瑪麗和迪肯感到很訝異。

pp. 66-67 「我下一個目標,是要跑贏迪肯。我們就來一較高下吧,我們來比賽,而且在比賽結束後,我們一定能變得更強壯。要是我贏了,那都是我們大家的成就,因為你們幫了我很多。然後呢,接下來的目標是要騎單車繞花園!」柯林雄心勃勃地說道。

「你現在看起來這麼有鬥志,一定會很厲害的。」迪肯說:「不過呢,我想你是休想跑贏我的。萬一你跑贏我,那我就叫我媽頒證書給你,如何?」

迪肯講這番話,並非是要諷刺柯林。經過了過去這幾個星期的相處,他們三個人已經變成了死黨。

他們哈哈大笑,知道迪肯不是想去挖苦柯林的能力,而不過是逗弄他一下而已。

一直到現在,除了瑪麗和迪肯,沒有人知道柯林已經能走路了。柯林想保守這個秘密,每當要回家時,他就叫迪肯幫他推輪椅。

這一天,他們在秘密花園裡休息時,瑪麗問柯林說:「你不想讓你爸爸知道你的身體現在都好了嗎?」

「我想讓他知道啊,不過我要給他一個大驚喜。」柯林說:「等他回來了,我就要讓他驚喜。」

瑪麗表示贊同,兩人真期待克雷文先生趕快回來。

8 給克雷文先生的大驚喜

pp. 68-69 這個春天，秘密花園和孩子們都充滿了活力，只可惜有個人活得死氣沈沈的，這個人就是亞齊伯‧克雷文，柯林的父親。

過去十年來，他到訪過歐洲許多美麗的地方，而他之所以出門旅遊，是因為他努力想忘掉家裡頭那些悲傷的事情。

他一直不斷地在尋找快樂，然而，他卻只是感到更憂鬱。他內心深處，愈來愈痛苦，愈來愈悲傷。

這一天，他人在奧地利境內的一條美麗溪河河畔。他望著河水，看著過身邊的花草樹木，一切顯得如此靜謐祥和。

他領會著眼前的美好景色，一陣睡意襲來，他進入了夢鄉。在夢裡，他聽到了亡妻的聲音。

「亞齊！亞齊！」

「親愛的！」克雷文先生在夢裡喊道：「你在哪裡？」

「我在花園裡呀！」聲音回答道。

克雷文先生從夢中醒來。他心想：「在花園裡？可是花園上了鎖，鑰匙也被埋起來了呀。」

克雷文先生望著溪水，又看看身邊美麗的花朵。眼前美麗的畫面，讓他想起了那座秘密花園，隨即他想到了柯林。

「我這父親真是糟糕透了！」他自言自語道。這麼多年來，他簡直完全忽略了柯林的存在。

pp. 70-71 他不敢看兒子，因為兒子會讓他痛苦地憶起亡妻。他只會趁柯林睡著時去看他。

「我真想柯林呀！」克雷文先生哭道：「我現在就要回家看我兒子，這個夢搞不好就是一個指示，要我趕快回家去。」

當克雷文先生回到家時，他看到梅管家一臉惶惑。

「主人啊，柯林變得跟以前都不一樣了呀。」梅管家說：「他現在看起來氣色好多了，而且白天有很多時間都待在戶外。瑪麗和瑪莎的弟弟迪肯，會推著他的輪椅四處走，而且還不准我們靠近他們。我好擔心啊，主人，他吃飯的胃口變得好大，而且起起伏伏的。他有時候不吃，有時又會吃很多東西，比一般健康的男孩還要吃得多。他人現在就在花園裡。」

「在花園裡。」這就是亡妻在夢裡頭對他說的話。

他急奔出門，往那座已經十年未曾去過的花園走去。他看到花園的門是關起來的，而且聽到裡面傳來孩童的嬉戲聲。就在他站在那裡聽著聲音時，門突然被打開，只見一個一般高的健康男孩跑出來，衝進他的懷裡。

「這，你……你是誰？」克雷文先生問道。

「是我啊，爸爸，我是柯林，你不認得我了嗎？」

「可是你……看起來不像啊。」

「是啊，爸爸，我自己也不敢相信啊。這簡直像魔法一樣，花園，瑪麗，迪肯，是他們讓我好起來的。爸爸，你看，我會活得很久很久喔，你很高興吧？」

pp. 72-73 克雷文先生緊緊摟著兒子，哭了起來。一方面，之前對兒子的冷落，讓他感到很自責；另一方面，他為柯林感到十分快樂。

一時之間，他說不出話來，隨即他想盡量保持平靜。

他對柯林說到：「柯林，我們一起進去花園裡吧，然後你再好好告訴我魔法的事。」

花園裡，玫瑰盛開，樹木高聳，知更鳥吱吱喳喳地叫著。孩子們跟克雷文先生說了自己的事，還有一些有趣的經歷。

克雷文先生時而哭泣，時而大笑，不過他大部分的時間都是凝視著寶貝兒子那張有點陌生卻很可愛的臉龐。

他簡直不敢相信，眼前這個健健康康的柯林以前曾經病得很重。這十年來，他第一次有了釋放的感覺。

黃昏時，當瑪麗、迪肯、柯林和克雷文先生走回屋子時，僕人都聚在門廊前迎接他們。

這時梅管家、瑪莎和其他僕人都驚訝得不得了，他們不斷揉著眼睛，迪肯推的輪椅上面竟然沒有人，而且小主人的背還挺得直直的，走路的步伐也很穩。

而更令人驚訝的是，房子的主人克雷文先生，他臉上竟然掛著燦爛的笑容。

梅管家邊流著淚，邊對瑪莎說：「主人回來了！他真的回來了！這就是我十年前所認識的那位紳士呀！」

Answers

Ch1 1. A 2. B 3. F 4. T 5. C 6. F

Ch2 1. F 2. B 3. F 4. C 5. T

Ch3 1. A 2. A
3. The robin hopped onto some old climbing ivy on the wall. Then somehow the ivy was blown aside by the wind and the door was found.

Ch4 4. c 5. F She used her allowance to cover the expenses.

Ch5 1. A 2. F 3. A 4. T

Ch6 1. B 2. B 3. A 4. B

1. B 2. A
3. Colin had always been told that either his back would become as crooked as his father's or he was sick and would die young.

Ch7 4. A 5. B

Ch8 1. T 2. C 3. C 4. B 5. F

1. C 2. F
3. Mr. Craven had become a happy and normal person, just like ten years ago.

Exercises

A 1. b 2. a 3. a 4. c 5. c 6. b 7. c 8. a 9. b 10. b
11. a 12. c 13. c 14. a 15. b

B 1. dressing 2. relocated 3. constantly 4. jump rope 5. treating

C 1. (1) out (2) by (3) with (4) in
2. (1) moor (2) vary (3) breathe (4) elsewhere
3. (1) undertaking (2) solid (3) demonstrated
   (4) resolution (5) unceasing

D 1. Mary looked closely at the plants and wondered if they were still alive.
2. For the past ten years, he had traveled to many beautiful places in Europe.

E 1. recounted 2. put forth 3. demanded 4. endorsed
5. claimed

國家圖書館出版品預行編目資料

秘密花園 = The Secret Garden / Frances Hodgson Burnett 著
; 鄭家文譯. -- 初版. --〔臺北市〕：寂天文化，2008.07　面；
公分. –

中英對照

ISBN 978-986-184-359-9 (25k 平裝附光碟片)

1. 英語　2. 讀本

805.18　　　　　　　　　　　　　　　　　97012386

秘密花園（中英對照）
The Secret Garden

Frances Hodgson Burnett	原著
Andrew Chien	改寫

編　　　譯	鄭家文	
主　　　編	黃鈺云	
審　　　訂	Dennis Le Boeuf / Liming Jing	
插　　　圖	高嘉玟	
製 程 管 理	林欣穎	
出　版　者	寂天文化事業股份有限公司	
電　　　話	02-2365-9739	
傳　　　真	02-2365-9835	
網　　　址	www.icosmos.com.tw	
讀 者 服 務	onlineservice@icosmos.com.tw	
出 版 日 期	2008 年 7 月　　　　初版一刷	250101
郵 撥 帳 號	1998620-0 寂天文化事業股份有限公司	

劃撥金額 900（含）元以上者，郵資免費。

訂購金額 900 元以下者，加收 60 元運費。

〔若有破損，請寄回更換，謝謝。〕